Curly McHoglet

Q: What do you get if you cross a
pig with itching powder?
A: Pork scratchings.

* * *

Q: Why don't piglets listen to
their fathers?
A: Because they are boars!

Queen Baabara

'Doctor, Doctor, i think i'm a shepherd!'
'Oh. i wouldn't lose any sheep over it!'

* * *

Q: How do sheep keep warm in
winter?
A: They turn on the central bleating.

SkyHog Jet 3

Q: What's a pilot's favourite food?
A: Chicken wings!

* * *

'Doctor, Doctor. i think i can fly.'
'Well, sit down and fasten your
seatbelt!'

Wolfie T. Wolfman

Q: What do you call a lost wolf?
A: A where-wolf.

* * *

Q: What grows on trees and is
scared of wolves?
A: The Three Little Figs.

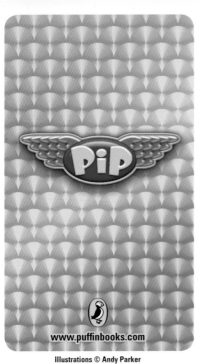

The Big Baad Sheep

Pigs CAN fly!

Kweeeeeeeeeeeeeeeeeeeeeeeeeep!

When the Alarm Squeal sounds it must
be a job for Captain Peter Porker and
the PIGS IN PLANES!

Paul Cooper is from Manchester.
He now lives in Cambridge with
his wife and two daughters.

*Read these high-flying adventures
about the Pigs in Planes:*

PIGS IN PLANES

The Big Baad Sheep

PAUL COOPER

Illustrated by Trevor Dunton

PUFFIN

PUFFIN BOOKS

Published by the Penguin Group
Penguin Books Ltd, 80 Strand, London WC2R 0RL, England
Penguin Group (USA) Inc., 375 Hudson Street, New York, New York 10014, USA
Penguin Group (Canada), 90 Eglinton Avenue East, Suite 700, Toronto, Ontario, Canada M4P 2Y3
(a division of Pearson Penguin Canada Inc.)
Penguin Ireland, 25 St Stephen's Green, Dublin 2, Ireland (a division of Penguin Books Ltd)
Penguin Group (Australia), 250 Camberwell Road, Camberwell, Victoria 3124, Australia
(a division of Pearson Australia Group Pty Ltd)
Penguin Books India Pvt Ltd, 11 Community Centre, Panchsheel Park, New Delhi – 110 017, India
Penguin Group (NZ), 67 Apollo Drive, Rosedale, North Shore 0632, New Zealand
(a division of Pearson New Zealand Ltd)
Penguin Books (South Africa) (Pty) Ltd, 24 Sturdee Avenue, Rosebank, Johannesburg 2196, South Africa

Penguin Books Ltd, Registered Offices: 80 Strand, London WC2R 0RL, England

puffinbooks.com

First published 2010
1

Text copyright © Paul Cooper, 2010
Illustrations copyright © Trevor Dunton, 2010
All rights reserved

The moral right of the author and illustrator has been asserted

Set in Bembo Infant
Made and printed in England by Clays Ltd, St Ives plc

British Library Cataloguing in Publication Data
A CIP catalogue record for this book is available from the British Library

ISBN: 978-0-141-32843-0

www.greenpenguin.co.uk

For Mathis

MEET THE CREW

TAMMY SNUFFLES,

Mechanic

BRIAN TROTTER,

Medical Officer

CURLY McHOGLET,

Trainee

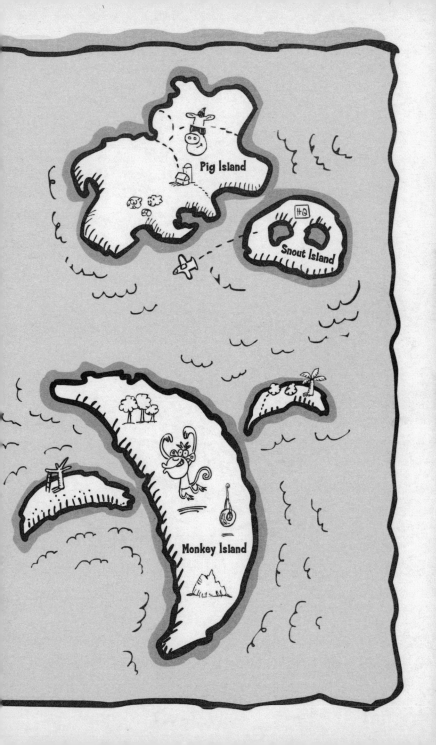

CHAPTER 1:

Ram Raid!

'Keep working!' ordered Wing Commander Peregrine Oinks-Gruntington. 'I want this floor clean enough to eat dinner off!'

'As medical officer, I'm not sure that would be wise,' Brian 'the Brain' Trotter answered as he scrubbed. 'It was vegetable soup for dinner today.'

Peregrine wanted everything to be perfect at the base because in two days' time the Air Chief Marshal of the entire PIAF (Pig Island Air Force) was going to visit the Pigs in Planes. The Wing Commander was already wearing his best uniform, despite the fact that it was at least three sizes too small.

'Let's hope our visitor's forgotten about last year's unfortunate incident with the tomato ketchup,' Peregrine said darkly.

'That wasn't my fault!' cried Tammy Snuffles, the PiPs mechanic, as she emptied the rubbish bin into a bag. 'You know I can't eat chips without ketchup, and that bottle had a really tricky lid! Anyway he shouldn't have been standing under the window.'

Peregrine continued to supervise by watching the team intently and munching on chocolate biccies. 'Wait a minute,' he said. 'Where's Peter?'

Curly McHoglet, the newest of the PiPs, looked up from his dusting. 'The captain's niece and nephew are visiting for the day,' he said. 'Pete's playing with them. They're next door – listen . . .'

Peregrine cocked his head. From the next

room came the sound of two little piglets' voices, laughing. Peregrine scowled.

'Captain Porker!' he shouted.

Moments later Pete's head appeared round the door. It was followed by two smaller heads, lower down.

'Please explain what you are doing,' Peregrine demanded.

Pete grinned, flashing his pearly-white choppers. 'No probs. I was just teaching little Rasher and Runt here my favourite song when I was their age.' He bent down to the little piglets. 'Do you want to show everyone?'

The two little piglets squealed with delight. They lined up with their uncle and all three began to sing at the top of their voices:

'I'm a little poopot,
Short and stout!
Here is my handle

For waving me about.
When I get all filled up
Hear me shout:
Don't kick me
Or poo will fly out!'

As they sang, they did all of the actions, ending by jumping up and throwing their arms in the air.

Peregrine's huge white moustache twitched crossly. In his opinion, children should be seen and not heard . . . and preferably not seen all that much either.

'Are you aware, Captain Porker, that in less than forty-eight hours a VIP – a Very Important Pig – will be visiting? You have duties and responsibilities other than messing around like a little piglet!'

Pete shrugged. 'I think it's important to connect with your inner piglet sometimes, sir. I'm talking about the piglet that you used to be years ago – *lots* of years ago, in your case. You ought to try it yourself. Come on, Peregrine. How about just one quick verse of "I'm a little poopot"? You know you want to . . .'

There were times when Pete showed a unique ability to get Peregrine worked up. Now was one of those times. If the Wing Commander *did* have an inner piglet, it was buried deep under a lot of angry adult pig.

'Why's that large pig turning purple?' asked little Rasher.

'Maybe he doesn't know the words,' suggested little Runt.

As the children helpfully began to bellow their song again, Peregrine did what he always did to calm down. He shoved another biccie into his mouth. But this final treat proved to be too much for the Wing Commander's overstretched suit. A shiny

brass button pinged off his jacket and shot out at high speed.

It hit Curly right in the ribs. 'OW!' the trainee PiP cried, hopping forward.

Curly's dusting feather jabbed Tammy in the side. 'OI!' the PiPs mechanic shouted, dropping her bag of rubbish on to the floor and bumping into Brian.

'OOF!' the PiPs medic gasped, falling sideways into his bucket and sending a pool of dirty water across the floor.

As Peregrine looked at the chaotic scene in front of him, his high hopes plummeted faster than a hot-air balloon after an unlucky encounter with a grumpy woodpecker. What chance did he stand of making a good impression on the Air Chief Marshal with this lot?

'Is the large pig going to explode?' asked little Runt.

'What will fly out if he does?' wondered little Rasher.

The Wing Commander could feel a scream building in his chest. He opened his mouth, but was beaten to it by a sound from the speakers on the wall:

'*KWEEEEEEEEEEEEEEEEEEEEEEEE-EEEEEEEEEEEEEEEEEEEEEEEEP!*'

It was the PiPs Alarm Squeal. Somewhere in Animal Paradise, there was an emergency.

'Quick! To the planes!' shouted Pete.

The members of the flight team pulled off

their aprons and rubber gloves and threw
down their cleaning gear. They raced for the
exit gratefully.

'Be good for Uncle Peregrine!' shouted
Pete to his niece and nephew as he headed
for the hangar.

Minutes later the PiPs had taken their
places in the three SkyHog jets and were
ready to take off.

'Where to?' Pete asked over the radio.

'You're going to Sheep Island,' replied
Lola Penn, the PiPs radio operator. 'OK,
cleared for take-off.'

Pete smiled. 'Not baad,' he said, chuckling
to himself. The scream of the jet engines
drowned out the other pigs' groans as Pete
hit the throttle and zoomed up into the dark
evening sky.

'PiPs are GO!' shouted Tammy.

Once they had all taken off and fallen
into formation, Lola explained the full

details of the mission over the radio.

'You all know about the Golden Fleece of Sheep Island, right?' she said.

'Er . . .' answered Pete.

Brian's voice piped up. 'According to legend, the Golden Fleece was given to the very first ruler of the island, Ramses I, thousands of years ago. It's been passed down to every sheep king or queen since then. If anything bad ever happens to the Golden Fleece, they say it will be a terrible disaster for the island.'

'Oh, OK, *that* Golden Fleece,' lied Pete. 'What's happened to it?'

'It's just been *stolen*,' answered Lola. 'Some Royal GrassEaters were transporting it in an unmarked truck —'

Tammy cut in. 'GrassEaters?'

'That's what the sheep guards at the Royal Tower are called,' explained Brian, who had read *1001 Woolly Royal Traditions* from cover to cover several times. 'The tradition dates back to –'

'We don't need a history lesson just now, Bri!' said Tammy.

'Anyway, a gang intercepted the truck,' continued Lola. 'They battered in the back doors and fled with the Fleece!'

'Sounds like a tough mission,' said Curly from his trainee seat in Pete's plane. 'Those ram raiders could be anywhere by the time we arrive!'

The three jets were approaching Sheep Island airspace now, but they were still a few minutes away from the capital, Woollyhampton.

'You're right, Curly, but there's an electronic tracking device sewn inside the Fleece,' Lola explained. 'I'll give you the right frequency and then you can follow the transmitter.'

The lights of Woollyhampton's outer

suburbs were coming into view below; the SkyHogs would be at the city centre any moment. Pete started looking for a place to land.

'So how come the GrassEaters can't just follow the signal themselves?' asked Curly.

Lola gave her answer careful thought. 'They ... said they found the tracking technology a little bit tricky to operate because ... Well, when it comes to brains,

sheep aren't exactly *three bags full*, if you
know what I mean.'

'Not really,' said Curly.

'Because sheep are stupid!' Pete cut in
with a laugh.

As the three jets came in to land, no one
disagreed.

CHAPTER 2:

A Prickly Situation

It didn't take long to land the SkyHog jets in
an empty car park and hit the ground. Brian
was already tuning in his trotter-held radio
to the right frequency for the tracking device.

While they waited, Tammy turned to
Curly. 'Erm, why are you wearing a tea cosy
on your head?' asked the mechanic.

'It's not a tea cosy,' said Curly indignantly,
running one trotter over the yellow and
purple garment. 'It's a woolly helmet cover.
My nan sent it. She knitted it for me, to keep
my head warm on missions. Do you like it?'

'It's, er . . . very fetching,' began Tammy.

'I like how it says "I
LOVE PiPs" on the
side.'

'Brilliant, isn't it?'
Curly gushed. 'I could
knit one for you too –
my nan taught me
how to knit, and
she sent me a set of

needles as well!' He patted his jacket pocket.
'I could make us all one! We could have
matching woollen helmet covers!'

Pete smiled. 'Sorry, kid. I don't *do* knitted
clothing.'

The radio in Brian's trotters let out a
beep. 'This way!' shouted the medical officer,
starting to run. The other PiPs followed. It
was late and the streets of Woollyhampton
were quiet. Any sheep that *were* out and
about soon dashed for cover when they saw
a scrum of uniformed pigs charging along.

After a few minutes they came to a deserted area of large warehouses and factories, all closed up for the night.

'I don't understand,' said Brian, peering at the tiny screen on his radio. 'If these coordinates are correct, the Golden Fleece should be right about . . . here?'

The four pigs scanned the dark, empty streets around them. There was nothing that looked very suspicious or at all Golden Fleece-y.

'Let's have a look at that thing,' said Pete, reaching for the radio receiver. He studied the signal. 'Hmm. Whoever's got the Fleece isn't even moving. So where is it? It can't have vanished into thin –' He paused, then looked up. 'Air! That's where it is!'

The captain started running towards the nearest building. 'Brian and Curly, you stay out here!' he shouted. 'Tammy, you come with me!'

'Where?' asked the mechanic.

'To the rooftops! The signal *is* coming from these coordinates, but not at ground level. It's *above* us!'

The building's front door was shut, but not many locks could stop Tammy Snuffles and her handy-dandy lock-busting hairpin. Moments later, they were inside the darkened lobby.

'You check the emergency stairs, Tammy,' said Pete. 'I'll take the lift up to the top floor.'

Tammy had to use a torch to light the darkened stairwell. She raced up to the first floor two steps at a time. She took a bit longer getting from the first floor to the second. By the time she'd reached the third flight, she had slowed down quite a bit. By the next flight of stairs, she was down to a steady plod.

She was grimly eyeing up the next flight, when she heard a noise. It came from

behind the door between the two flights
of stairs. With no time to call for back-up,
Tammy gripped the handle and pushed
open the door.

She stepped out into a dark corridor and
pointed her torch into the gloom. A large
figure loomed in a doorway.

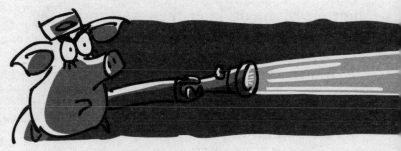

'Step into the light, pal, and don't try
anything silly!' Tammy yelled. 'Now where's
the Fleece?' She shone the torch, but all she
could see were two large yellow eyes staring
out of the darkness.

'Who are you?' demanded Tammy, but
the shadowy figure gave no answer. Instead,
in a deep, rich voice, it said, 'Look deep into
the eyes.'

'Yeah, right,' said Tammy, and yet somehow she found herself unable to break the spell of those eyes. It seemed as if they were getting bigger and bigger, until she could see nothing else. Those yellow eyes in the dark were like pools of custard, and the PiPs mechanic felt herself falling in.

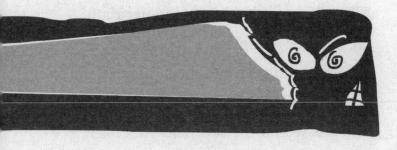

Meanwhile Pete was opening a door out on to the building's flat rooftop. According to the tracker readings, the Golden Fleece should be here. The captain crept out of the little hut the stairs had ended in, edged along with his back to the wall, and then wheeled round the corner, adopting a deadly Kung-Poo stance.

There was no fleece, but Pete could see a little electronic device sitting on the ground. The transmitter! The thieves must have removed it from the Fleece.

Hoping that he wasn't too late, Pete rushed round the next corner . . . and found himself face to face with a skinny sheep. Well, it was probably no skinnier than the average sheep, but it looked this way because it had recently been sheared. In one hoof it carried a fleece, but Pete was pretty sure this wasn't the sheep's own. This fleece was oddly *golden-coloured* . . .

'Stop right there, *Ram-bo!*' shouted Pete. 'You're under arrest!'

The shorn sheep did not reply. It didn't even look at him, or give any reaction at all. Instead it ran smoothly up the pitched roof that covered the main part of the building, then trotted unhurriedly along the ridge at the top. It showed no signs of fear or panic.

Pete began to scramble up the sloping roof after it. The surface was slippery and he almost fell several times. How had the sheep managed it so easily?

Must be a professional, Pete thought.

He began to tiptoe carefully along the ridge after the fleeing fleece-napper. It was harder than it looked, and the street was a long way down. Pete didn't want to end the day as a ham pizza, but he didn't want the sheep to get away either. He made his way past a skylight in the roof. He peeked down into the dimly lit main area of the building and smiled grimly when he saw the sign on the wall:

SUPERSOFT, SLUMBERTIME MATTRESSES

Underneath the sign, dozens of mattresses were stacked high. If he *did* fall, at least there'd be something soft to land on.

He looked ahead and saw that the sheep

was nearing the end of the roof. There was nowhere for it to go!

'Got you!' Pete smiled to himself.

But the sheep didn't stop, or even slow down. It *speeded up,* racing to the edge of the roof, and then leapt off. The warehouse was separated from the next by a narrow alley, and the sheep jumped across the gap like a trained athlete. It landed gracefully, then carried calmly along the next rooftop.

Gritting his teeth, Pete also speeded up and he too leapt across the gap to the next building. He landed in a heap. It knocked the breath out of him, but there was no time to rest.

The PiPs captain made his way up to the

next ridge, and he continued to follow the sure-footed sheep. This second roof had a skylight as well. As he passed it, Pete peered into the warehouse below. There was a sign on the wall here too:

FUNTIME BOUNCY TRAMPOLINES

If he *did* fall, at least he might bounce his way to safety.

Pete glanced ahead and saw that the runaway sheep was picking up speed once more. The gap to the next building was even wider, but again the sheep didn't hesitate. It calmly leapt across and continued its escape.

Pete knew he couldn't keep this up much longer – it was now or never. He threw all of his energy into a final sprint, leaping across the gap. But he was moving too fast to control his landing. Arms flailing wildly, he high-stepped madly across the next rooftop. Before his legs gave out from under him, he flung himself at the sheep.

He managed to catch its back leg with one trotter and both animals tumbled towards this building's skylight. They crashed through it in a shower of glass.

As they plunged downwards, the sign on the wall was just a blur to Pete. He had only a moment to wonder at what was inside this large building. Pillows? Foam packing? Inflatable dinghies?

Then they landed and Pete found out the hard way what the sign on this wall said:

COLIN'S CACTUS WAREHOUSE

A few minutes later, following the sound of all the yelping, Brian and Curly made their way to the cactus warehouse.

'Are you OK, Pete?' asked Curly

anxiously. 'We heard you from three blocks away.'

Pete yelped as he plucked another cactus needle out of his bum. As the PiPs medical officer, Brian was usually responsible for all medical emergencies, but he decided to let the captain get on with the task himself on this particular occasion.

'That sheep got even more prickles than me,' said Pete, 'but he never even made a sound. It's as if he didn't feel any pain, like he was some sort of robot or something. He just got up and raced off before I could grab him.'

'I imagine he took the Golden Fleece with him?' asked Brian, taking care to keep his eyes above waist level.

Pete grinned through the pain. He reached up behind him and pulled a sparkly object from the cactus limb it had snagged on to. Close up, it looked a bit cheap and shiny, but it was definitely the Golden Fleece.

'You've got it!' cried Tammy, joining the other PiPs in the cactus warehouse. 'What happened?'

Pete explained quickly, skipping over the bit about needles in his backside.

'How about you?' he asked. 'Did you find anything in the stairwell?'

Tammy thought for a moment, as if she was trying to remember something. 'No,' she said, 'there was nothing there . . . Nothing there at all.'

CHAPTER 3:

No More Mr Nice Pig

Pete couldn't walk too fast, so it was really late when the PiPs got back to the parked SkyHogs. They radioed Peregrine to let him know the Fleece was in safe trotters.

'Good work,' said the Wing Commander. 'But you can't fly home and go to bed just yet. Your mission isn't over. As you know, the Golden Fleece is usually kept safe in a vault at the Royal Tower.'

Pete glanced at the golden wool hanging over the nose of Tammy's jet and sniffed. 'They should probably take it to a launderette every so often,' he whispered.

'However, once every year, the Queen
of Sheep Island must wear it for the
official opening of Baaliament,' continued
Peregrine. 'That ceremony takes place
tomorrow afternoon.'

'Er, what's *Baaliament*?' asked Curly.

'It's the sheep's government building,'
said Brian. 'Every year there's a big royal
procession and ceremony when the Queen
re-opens it after a break.'

'Quite so,' said Peregrine. 'Which means
that the Fleece cannot go back to the Tower
until after the ceremony. But . . . we believe

the same gang of ruthless criminals may try to steal the Fleece again. PiPs, your mission is to keep the Fleece safe at all costs. The first robbery attempt may have been an inside job, so assume that you can trust no one. Brian and Tammy – I want you to keep the Fleece safe and take it to Flockingham Palace first thing in the morning.'

Peregrine went on to explain the plan in detail, but Brian wasn't really listening. He was too excited.

'We're going to meet the Queen!' he cried.

Tammy rolled her eyes. 'Great!' she moaned.

★ ★ ★

Pete was pacing around the parked SkyHogs trying to think of any leads that might help him find the sheep he had chased across the rooftops.

'Would you recognize him if you saw him again?' Curly asked, as the captain passed him for the ninth time.

Pete rubbed his chin. 'He'd had his fleece completely sheared off, and that makes it hard to tell sheep apart. Of course, there is *one* identifying feature . . . He got quite a few cactus prickles in his backside.' He smiled grimly. 'But a hardened, top-level professional criminal like that wouldn't pop along to the hospital just to have a few prickles pulled out, now, would he?'

He continued to pace around the planes. When he'd completed another circuit, he saw that Curly was talking into his mobile phone. 'OK, OK, thank you . . .'

The young pig looked up proudly. 'I just called the local hospital. They say a sheep came into their Emergency Ward half an hour ago with a load of cactus prickles sticking out of him.'

It was the middle of the night when Pete and Curly got to the hospital. The suspect was still in an examination room. He had given his name to the nurse as 'Greg Dagley', but Pete was sure this had to be a fake name. He called Lola quickly.

'Sorry, were you sleeping?' he asked.

'No, what, YES . . . why?' mumbled Lola, who never left her desk during a mission.

'It's just that you were still snoring when you picked up the phone,' said Pete. He asked her to run a computer check on the sheep's name.

After he hung up, Pete peeked through the blinds into the examination room. That was the same sheep all right, the one that had leapt from building to building so fearlessly.

'Better let me do the talking,' Pete told Curly.

As usual, Curly was eager to help. 'Ooh, can I have a go at asking questions, Pete?' he asked. 'Can I? Huh?'

'I don't know, kid. This is one tough customer, a ruthless professional. He won't crack easily.'

'I can do it, I know I can!' said Curly.

Pete looked into the young pig's eager eyes. 'OK, kid. You can give it a go. But listen – you've got to be tough. Don't show any sign of weakness.'

Curly gave a determined nod. He had never interviewed a suspect before, but he *had* watched lots of films. He'd show Pete he could do it – he'd be the toughest investigator ever!

When the two pigs entered the room,

'Greg' did a good job of pretending to look confused.

'Can I go home now?' he began. 'My bum's all better.'

'You're not going anywhere,' barked Curly in his best tough-pig voice, 'until you start squawking!'

'Squawking? Er ...'

Curly tried again. 'Um. You heard me . . .
Spill the beans!'

Greg the sheep blinked. 'I don't really like
beans. I prefer grass . . .'

This wasn't going very well for Curly. He
tried one more time. 'We need information
so just . . . start singing!'

Puzzled, the sheep cleared his throat and,
in a wobbly voice, began to bleat the first
line of a recent pop song, 'Flock 'n' Roll
Star'.

Pete put a trotter on Curly's shoulder.
'That's terrific,' he whispered to the trainee,
'but maybe you're being a bit *too* tough.
Take it down a little, eh?'

Curly nodded – acting tough didn't
really come naturally to him; he was much
happier being nice. He smiled at the sheep
now. 'So anyway, Greg? I hope your bum
is feeling better now. They said you looked
like a giant hedgehog when you first got

here.' He reached into his pocket. 'Would you like a sweetie? It's my last one, but you can have it. What are your hobbies, by the way? I like knitting, watching cartoons and playing football . . . Not all at the same time, obviously.'

Pete took hold of Curly's arm and whispered into his ear again. 'I think maybe you've gone a bit too far the other way. Actually, can I just ask him a quick question?'

Pete turned to the sheep. Over the years the PiPs captain had learnt to trust his gut instincts, and right now his gut was telling him that it was time for breakfast. And also that this sheep was *not* the criminal sort.

'Can you tell us how you got all of those cactus prickles?' he asked.

'I . . . don't know,' Greg bleated.

'OK, then just tell us what happened yesterday.'

Greg nodded. 'It's shearing time, so I went to get my fleece cut. Then I went straight home. After that, I can't remember anything. The next thing I knew, I woke up in the street. It was late at night and I had loads of cactus needles in my behind!'

It made no sense, and yet Pete found himself believing this sheep's story. He just couldn't imagine someone like Greg leading him on such a high-speed, high-danger chase.

A moment later Lola texted to say that all of Greg's details checked out. He didn't work for a ruthless gang of criminals; he worked in a sweet shop. But Pete didn't need Lola to tell him this. His gut was letting him know that this sheep was telling the truth. But how could that be?

A thought popped into his head. 'Where did you go to get your fleece cut off?' he asked.

'It's a new shearing salon, called SHEAR DELIGHT,' said Greg. 'It's not too far from the palace.'

Pete stroked his chin. 'Maybe we need to check out this salon, Curly.'

'Like a real investigation?' Curly asked eagerly.

'Yep.'

'Brilliant! Should we radio Brian and Tammy to let them know?'

Pete glanced at his watch. It would soon be sunrise. 'Let's see if we find any clues before calling them,' he said. 'Anyway, pretty soon they'll be on their way to the Palace to visit the Queen.'

The sun hadn't been up long when Tammy and Brian arrived at Flockingham Palace. They followed a royal servant down one of the many long corridors, past all the portraits of old sheep monarchs in their finest robes of wool. Although the PiPs hadn't had much sleep, Brian could hardly contain his excitement at being here.

Tammy was less impressed. 'How many bedrooms has this place got, anyway?'

'Three hundred and sixteen,' said Brian dreamily.

'And how many members of the royal family live here?'

'Two . . . The Queen, and her son, Prince Larry.'

Tammy thought this over. 'Bet he has some killer sleepover parties.'

The servant opened a door at the end of the corridor and waved the pigs inside. 'Her Majesty will be with you shortly,' he said.

The room was full of valuable antiques and there were priceless paintings hanging on the velvet flock wallpaper. Brian allowed himself a gigantic smile. 'I've always been a bit of a royal spotter,' he confessed.

'Tell me something
I don't know,' said
Tammy. 'You put up a
calendar of the Royal
Families of Animal
Paradise in the common
room . . . AND you
got miffed when
someone threw a
dart at the King of
Cow Island's picture.'

'It hit him right in
the eye!' said Brian.

Tammy grinned
proudly. 'Exactly –
bullseye!' She went to
sit in one of the plush
armchairs.

'Erm, I don't think
you should sit there!'
cried Brian.

Tammy straightened up. 'Why not?'

'Well . . . you might get it mucky.'

Tammy raised an eyebrow. 'Are you saying my flightsuit is dirty?'

'Er . . . yes,' said Brian. 'Obviously.'

Tammy peeked back at the mix of engine oil, floorwax and popcorn butter on the back of her flightsuit. 'Oh right . . . Good point.'

CHAPTER 4:

A Pig in Sheep's Clothing

'How do I look?' Curly asked.

Pete walked around the trainee PiP, carefully studying the fleece he was now wearing on top of his flightsuit. They were in an alleyway round the corner from the SHEAR DELIGHT shearing salon.

'You look . . .' Pete knew Curly would spot *brilliant* or even *good* as outright lies. '. . . OK?'

'But do I look like a sheep?'

'You look *sheepish*.' Pete crossed his arms. 'I mean, to you or me, you look like a pig wearing a cheap fleece. But, as you now know, your average sheep isn't so bright. They'll never notice, so long as you throw in a few *baas* here and there and look like you're chewing something! Just get in there, have a good look for anything suspicious, and then get out. Shouldn't take more than about fifteen minutes, tops.'

Curly's expression was a mix of determination and anxiety.

'You'll be fine, kid,' said Pete. He patted his own ample belly. 'I'd do it myself, but I'm too big-boned to pass for a sheep.' He pointed to a window on the first floor of the building opposite the salon.

'I'll be right up there, watching everything. If there's a problem, I'll be over like a shot.' He winked. 'Don't worry, Curly – Captain Peter Porker never sleeps on the job!'

By the time Curly reached the front door of the SHEAR DELIGHT salon, he was feeling better about his disguise. He had passed several sheep in the street, and none had given him a second glance.

Inside the shop, the ewe on the reception desk didn't look up from her magazine – *GrassLovers' World*, with its lead article '101 Easy Grass Recipes for the Sheep on the Go'.

'Cubicle sixteen,' she told Curly in a lifeless voice.

As the PiPs trainee made his way to the shearing cubicle, he looked for clues. He didn't have much idea what these might be. All they knew was that a normal, average sheep had come here the day before, and *something* had turned him into a fearless criminal.

Curly could see shelf after shelf of fleece-care products – shampoos and dyes, curlers, crimpers and straighteners, sheep-tick powder, and so on. It didn't look as if these

received much use –
there was a layer of
dust on them all.

On the wall, there
was a poster showing
all of the different
fleece styles available.
At different times,
various styles had
been the 'in' look on
Sheep Island – the
Poodle, the Lightning
Strike (in which the
fleece was made to
stand on end), the Mr
Whippee Ice-cream
Scoop – but these cuts
had all been crossed
off. The only item
remaining was:

No. 1 Buzz Cut

Hmm, thought Curly. *You'd think a proper salon would offer more than one cut.*

Once he went into the narrow cubicle, a heavy door closed behind him. Inside there was nothing more suspicious than a large shearing chair. Curly sat, knowing he'd have to leave before it was time for his fleececut.

But, as soon as his backside hit the chair, there was a click and a whirr, then a violent jerk as the chair tipped backwards. It began to roll back and down, but it didn't hit the floor, because part of the floor was missing – it was a trapdoor! And Curly and the entire shearing chair were dropping right through it!

At Flockingham Palace, Brian stood at one of the room's tall windows.

The Queen's massed marching band were outside practising. They had played 'Mary was a Little Lamb' umpteen times, but they still hadn't made it all the way to the end without mistakes.

Even Brian, who had a wide collection of military brass music, found it hard to listen to.

'They're not much good, are they?' he said.

'Not much good?' echoed Tammy. 'They're complete and utter –'

'Shh!' hissed Brian. 'We're in Flockingham Palace! You have to be on your best behaviour! And that also means no burping or tooting . . .'

Suddenly the door handle rattled. The two pigs looked expectantly at the door, but it didn't open.

'We are having some difficulty with the handle!' came an astonishingly posh voice from the other side of the door.

Tammy rolled her eyes. 'Try turning it, missus!'

'Who's there?' asked Brian.

'Our Royal Majesty, Queen Baabara of

Sheep Island,' replied the voice regally.

'Let me get the door for you!' cried Brian. He started across the room, but Tammy was moving to cut him off.

'Er, what are you doing, Tammy?' the medic asked. 'I've got to let the Queen in.'

Tammy lifted her trotters and grabbed Brian round the neck. She began to squeeze.

'Erm, Tammy, that thing about burping and tooting . . . it was just a friendly reminder!' choked Brian.

Tammy tightened her grip.

'Steady on!' exclaimed Brian, trying to pull her off. 'If it's about your dirty flightsuit, I'm sorry –'

Tammy still didn't speak. She stared forward blankly and continued to throttle her team-mate.

Brian was aware of the awful music still playing outside and the rattle of the door handle, but spots were beginning to appear in front of his eyes. What had got into the PiPs mechanic? Who knew that Tammy was so sensitive? Then again, who knew that Tammy was so *strong*?

Suddenly the handle caught and the door swung open. A small sheep with a huge fleece of fine wool and a prim little handbag swept regally into the room. It was Queen Baabara. A small crown was perched on top of her head.

The Queen didn't seem to notice that one of her guests was trying to kill the other – or she was too polite to mention it. She looked crossly at the door handle. 'We are NOT amused,' she declared. Then she turned to the pigs: 'We are delighted to make your acquaintance.'

As soon as the Queen appeared, Tammy jerked back as if she'd been given an electric shock. She let go of Brian's neck and turned to the Queen with a smile. Curtsies weren't really Tammy's style, so she gave the Queen a thumbs up and said, 'Wotcha, Maj!'

Brian held his throat in disbelief and croaked a hello.

'What's wrong with your voice, Bri?' asked Tammy innocently. 'I've got a throat lozenge somewhere.' She fished it out of her pocket and picked the protective layer of hairs off.

'You just tried to strangle me!' Brian protested.

'Huh?' Tammy patted the medical officer's back. 'You're imagining things, Bri.' She turned to the Queen. 'He can be a bit *dramatic,*' she whispered.

Brian blinked in confusion. Tammy was acting as if she *hadn't* just tried to kill him! What was going on? Was she ill? Was *he* ill?

Queen Baabara peered at the pigs as if she needed her glasses. (In fact, she looked at everything with this slightly puzzled gaze.)

'If you're *quite* finished,' she proclaimed, 'we believe there are important matters to discuss. You may take royal breakfast with us.' She turned to leave.

Tammy elbowed her team-mate and whispered, 'Why does she keep saying "we"?'

Brian elbowed his team-mate back and whispered, 'The Queen never refers to herself as "I". It's called the "Royal we".'

'I might need a royal wee soon,' said
Tammy. 'I drank too much tea this
morning!'

Normally Brian would be horrified.
But his mind was on other things as
they followed the Queen into the Royal
Breakfast Room. He rubbed his sore neck
and wondered what on earth was going on.

Sitting in the window across the street from
the SHEAR DELIGHT shearing salon, Pete
waited.

And waited.

He looked at his watch. Then he waited
some more. It had been four minutes since
Curly had set off on his mini-mission, but
it felt like four hours to Pete. No, make that
four weeks. No wonder he felt peckish.

He lifted his binoculars again. He had
seen Curly go into one of the salon's little

shearing cubicles, but nothing after that. Pete checked his watch again – he'd give the trainee five minutes to reappear.

Until then there was nothing to do apart from watch all the sheep wander by on the street. Pete stifled a yawn with the back of his trotter. He'd always wondered why some animals counted sheep to help them get to sleep. Personally whenever he had trouble nodding off, Pete liked to count all the ways that he himself was one cool pig. The list generally started:

1. Looks cool in shades.

2. Looks cool in swimwear.

3. Has never owned a cardigan.

Pete had never got beyond number 3 before drifting off with a contented smile on his chops.

But as he watched the sheep walking past now like little ground-based clouds, he had to admit that there was something about the sight that made him pleasantly drowsy. He decided to count how many sheep were walking in either direction.

One . . .

Two . . .

ZZZZZZZZZZZZZZZZZZZZZZZ!

CHAPTER 5:
Blades of Grass and Blades of Steel

Curly was still in the shearing chair, but the chair was no longer in the cubicle – it had dropped into a large, open basement area. Curly looked from side to side and saw lots of other shearing chairs around him. Each one held a sheep, and all of the sheep were blankly staring forward. There was a fair bit of drooling going on too.

They were all looking at a big screen, which provided the only light in this gloomy space. It showed an ever-turning pattern of swirling spirals and, in front of this, a giant pair of glowering yellow eyes.

A booming voice was saying the same words again and again over a speaker system:

'You are feeling very, very sleepy! Do not move. Stay in your seats, sheep!'

There was *something* about this voice that made Curly want to obey. It suddenly seemed a wonderful idea just to stay put here. Perhaps have a little nap?

It was only when the voice said the word 'sheep' that a tiny part of Curly's brain

piped up: 'Oi, you're not a sheep, matey! Get on your trotters and get out of here!'

Feeling as if his arms and legs weighed a ton, Curly forced himself to move. He scurried towards the only door in sight. With a bit of luck it would lead to a staircase back up to ground level. He *had* to run and tell Pete about this place.

He pulled the door open, and looked down at a mop and bucket inside a little closet. Curly sighed – even dangerous criminal operations had to keep the place neat and tidy, he supposed.

Suddenly from behind him came a new noise. Was it footsteps? Curly didn't wait to find out. He crammed himself into the broom cupboard and pulled the door partly closed.

Peeking through the gap, he saw a couple of burly rams. None of the seated sheep paid them any attention; all eyes were still fixed on the screen.

The voice on the speaker system was saying, 'Listen carefully, sheep. After shearing, you will be given instructions. Follow these instructions exactly. When your task is over, you will wake up. The last thing you will remember is getting a fleececut and then going straight home. Do you understand?'

There was a chorus of drowsy *baa*s in response to this. Then the two big rams began to lead sheep one by one out of their chairs and over to the far end of the room.

Curly watched in horror. So *that's* why a normal sheep like Greg had acted like a master criminal. He had been *hypnotized*! And the same thing was happening now to all of these sheep! They had come to get sheared, and now they were all getting hypnotized. No doubt they were being given secret instructions to commit crimes like stealing the Golden Fleece! Curly had to admit, it was brilliantly evil. Whoever was behind all this was able to create an army of slaves who would mindlessly carry out crime.

Suddenly a tinkling electronic noise filled the broom closet, playing 'Piggy Sue' by Buddy Hoggy and the Piglets – it was his mobile phone! He'd forgotten to set it to silent!

As he dug frantically into his pocket, his trotter bumped the Talk button. 'Curly! How's my favourite little PiPster?' shouted the voice from the phone. 'This is your nan, just calling to see if you liked the woolly hat and needles I sent you? Did you –'

Curly jabbed End Call. He quickly turned the phone off before his furious nan called back to give him a pig's-earful.

He peeked out of the door again. Had anyone heard? The rams were still herding hypnotized sheep out of the room. Maybe he was still safe . . .

But then Curly became aware of a
large shape approaching from the side. The
outline looked like a sheep, but an enormous
one. Curly jerked the door shut and held his
breath in the dark.

After a few seconds, there came a
gentle tap-tap-tapping on the door.
The same deep voice that had been
on the speaker system now cooed,
'Little piggy, little piggy, let me in,
let me in . . .'

Curly didn't know what to say.
After all, he didn't have any hairs on
his chinny-chin-chin.

★ ★ ★

In the Royal Breakfast Room at Flockingham
Palace, the Queen took a seat at one end
of a long table. Brian and Tammy sat at the
other.

Normally, Brian would have been excited
to be here with a real-life queen, but today
was different. His mind was racing. What was
wrong with Tammy? He wanted to get out
of here as quickly as possible and run some
tests on her.

The Queen gazed the length of the table
at them. 'Kindly explain how you intend
to keep the Golden Fleece safe for us,' she
commanded.

Brian nodded, eager to do this quickly.
'Well, you usually travel to the Opening
Ceremony in the royal limousine, ma'am.
Today the limo will go the same as usual, but
you won't be inside it. The car is just going
to be a decoy, while the PiPs take you to the

Houses of Baaliament a different way.'

The Queen appeared to be deep in thought. Finally she said, 'We have no idea what you just said, but we are sure that will be fine.'

'Great!' said Brian, getting up. 'In that case we'll be on our way ...'

The Queen raised an imperious hoof. 'Not until you have taken breakfast, surely?'

'But –' Brian knew this was a great honour, but he just wanted to get Tammy out of there in case she had another one of her funny spells and tried to strangle Queen Baabara.

But Tammy was already tying a napkin round her neck. 'Brill!' she said. 'I'm starving!'

Brian sat down again. 'Thank you,' he sighed. 'That would be lovely.'

Moments later, with a clack of hooves on marble floors, the royal servants brought shining platters to the table. They lifted the silver lids with a flourish.

Tammy looked down at her food, blinked, and then looked up, a blank expression on her face. For a horrible moment, Brian thought she was about to attack again. In fact, she was just puzzled about the food on her plate.

'It's grass,' she said.

At the other end of the table, Queen Baabara was already bending and slurping grass into her mouth. With no knives and forks in sight, the pigs were expected to do the same.

'It's rude not to eat it!' whispered Brian.

He scooped some grass up with his tongue.

'But . . . it's grass!' said Tammy.

'We can't help noticing that you are not eating,' called Queen Baabara. 'Is everything all right?'

'Fine, thank you, Your Majesty,' answered Brian through a forced grin. He dropped his voice to an urgent whisper, desperate to get this meal over and done with. 'Just EAT your breakfast, Tammy!'

'But . . . it's . . . GRASS!'

While the Queen was bending her head for more, Brian grabbed a mound of grass from Tammy's plate and shoved it into his mouth. He began to chew. And chew.

It was a long, hard meal.

Finally Brian swallowed his last mouthful. 'Delicious, Your Majesty! Now we really must –'

Again, the Queen raised a hoof in command. 'The meal is not over until we have ruminated.'

She began to stare vacantly into space. The only sound came from outside, as the marching band continued to make a terrible din.

'What's she doing?' hissed Tammy, nodding at the Queen.

'She's *ruminating*,' replied Brian.

'What, *thinking*?' asked Tammy.

'No, actually ruminating – it's what sheep do with their food,' said Brian. 'Once they've softened the grass up in their stomachs, they bring it up again and chew it some more.'

'Gross,' sniffed Tammy.

For Brian the minutes seemed to crawl

by. Finally the Queen swallowed for the last time. 'Yummy,' she declared.

The PiPs medic leapt to his trotters, grateful that they had reached the end of the meal without any terrible incidents.

'Well, we must be going now, Your Majesty –'

Suddenly the door was flung open and a young ram charged into the room. Brian recognized him immediately – it was Prince Larry, the Queen's son and heir to the throne. The prince's large and stylishly fluffy fleece fluttered with indignation.

'Mummy!' he cried. 'Is it true? Are you really getting *pigs* to conduct important sheep business?'

'The Pigs in Planes are assisting us, yes.'

'But MUMMY!' whined Prince Larry. 'We can take care of it! I could lead a troop of GrassEaters! I was in the army, remember? OK, I dropped out after three days, but I did a lot of training in those three days.' He pointed a hoof at the two pigs. 'I don't care if they're Animal Paradise's "finest crime-fighting team". They're *pigs*! Smelly, dirty *pigs*!'

'Oi, who are you calling dirty?' said Tammy. 'I had a bath two weeks ago, matey.'

'You will refer to me as "Your Royal Highness, Prince Larry"!' screamed the prince, stamping his hoof. 'And you must refer to my mother as "Your Royal Majesty, Queen Baabara"!"

Brian didn't know what to say to this. Outside the marching band had turned their attention to 'Baa, Baa, Royal Sheep'. It wasn't any better than their last song. Brian edged towards the door. 'Well, OK, we'll just leave you and Prince Larry to it, Your Majesty. Come on, Tammy.'

But Tammy didn't reply. Instead she strode across the room and reached up to where two crossed swords were mounted over a shield on the wall. She pulled one curved sword down and began to slash the air threateningly. It made the sort of WHOOSHING noise train doors might make if they could chop your head off.

'Get away from me!' bleated Prince Larry, running to hide behind his mother. 'I've had army training, you know.'

But Tammy didn't care about the prince. She was looking only at Brian. When she spoke, her voice sounded flat and lifeless:

'Kill the pig!'

CHAPTER 6:

Who's Afraid of the Big Baad Sheep?

As a fully trained PiP, Brian knew how to keep his head in a crisis. He took one glance at the sharp look in Tammy's eyes and the even sharper sword in her trotter, and yelled 'WAH!' As Tammy charged towards him, he ran around the long table in the middle of the room.

'Look!' scoffed Prince Larry, shuffling out from behind his mother. 'This is who you want to trust!'

'Um, it's all OK, Your Majesty!' Brian cried desperately, managing to keep one step ahead of Tammy and her flashing blade. 'Just . . . a demonstration of what we can do!'

Behind him Tammy slashed with the sword again. This time she sliced open the back of Brian's flightsuit. Realizing that he couldn't outrun her much longer, Brian whirled round and grabbed a platter lid from the table. He used this as a shield and blocked the sword's next two thrusts. Tammy just pressed her attack harder, slashing in time to the music from outside, which got faster as it neared the end of the song.

'OK, I think that's enough, Tammy!' cried Brian, still trying to convince the royals that nothing was wrong.

'We agree! Those lids are the property of the Crown,' said Queen Baabara.

Tammy slashed again, knocking the lid out of Brian's hand. He had no way of protecting himself now. And he'd backed himself into a corner – there was nowhere to run. Tammy drew her arm back, ready for another thrust. Brian shut his eyes and –

'We said that is ENOUGH!' declared the Queen. 'We are NOT amused!'

– nothing happened.

Brian opened his eyes. Tammy was looking at the sword in her trotter in surprise. 'How did this get here?' she said casually. She shrugged and put the weapon down on a chair. 'Come on, Bri. Let's go!'

Both royal sheep just watched as she left the room.

'Well, I . . . er, hope our little demonstration has convinced you that we're the pigs for the job,' Brian said.

'We believe we got the point,' replied Queen Baabara haughtily.

As he followed Tammy, Brian thought to himself: *It was nearly ME who got the point – the point of a sword right through my bellybutton!* It seemed it was no longer just the Golden Fleece that needed protection.

In the basement beneath SHEAR DELIGHT, the huge sheep with the deep voice and the piercing yellow eyes studied Curly with a wolfish grin.

It was certainly an odd-looking sheep. Its snout seemed much longer than usual; its teeth were too long and pointy to be much good at chewing all the grass that sheep loved so much. Its eyes were a shade of yellow that might look quite nice on the walls of a small downstairs bathroom but which was a bit scary when staring straight at you.

'Let me introduce myself,' the gigantic sheep growled. 'The name is Wolfie T. Wolfman.'

'What does the "T" stand for?' asked Curly.

'It stands for *The* . . . It's an old family name.'

Wolfman tapped his unusually long snout. 'Big noses run in my family. All the better for sniffing out pigs who creep into my salon in disguise.'

A terrible thought was beginning to tickle Curly's brainbox. Something seemed out of place here. He was a PiP now, and it was a PiP's job to look beyond ordinary appearances, to spot the clues other animals might not see.

'Wait a minute . . .' he said. 'You're . . .'

'Ye-es?' said Wolfman patiently.

'You're not a real . . .'

'Spit it out!'

The truth hit Curly. 'You're not A REAL HAIRDRESSER!' he accused. 'Are you?'

'Oh, good grief!' snapped Wolfie T. Wolfman. 'And I thought *sheep* were stupid . . .' He reached down to a zip on the side of his fleece and began to pull.

'*Your* fleece isn't real either!' The truth hit Curly (again). 'So . . . you're BALD! Is that why you want the Golden Fleece? Because you have no wool?'

Wolfman stepped out of *his* sheep costume and the real, *actual* one hundred per cent truth hit Curly!

'You're a WOLF! A wolf in sheep's clothing!' he cried. 'Well, actually a wolf in a top-of-the-range, zip-up sheep disguise. And you're using this salon as a front to

hypnotize sheep and make them commit crimes!'

'How intelligent of you . . . eventually!' Wolfman turned the full glare of his yellow eyes on Curly.

Curly looked away. 'You're not going to hypnotize me!'

Wolfman's grin grew even wider. 'Why would I need to hypnotize you? I've got other plans for *you*, little pig.'

Pete was just waking up from his nap. He'd been having a great dream in which he'd been on the beach, playing volleyball in his cool Speedio trunks and even cooler mirror shades. Then the dream had turned bad when some of the pigs had started laughing, and Pete had looked down to see that he was now wearing a big woolly jumper with a teddy bear on the front.

He came awake with a start.

He looked at his watch – oh no! It had been over an hour since Curly had gone undercover into SHEAR DELIGHT. He ought to have come out by now.

Pete rushed down the stairs and across the road. Moments later he was pushing the salon door open. There was nobody on the reception desk now – in fact, there was nobody around at all.

'Curly?' he called, moving along the rows of empty shearing cubicles.

No answer. The bristles on the back of Pete's neck stood on end. Where could the trainee have gone? Pete knew one thing – he would rip this place apart, if that's what it took to find the trainee.

Just then his phone rang. It was Curly!

'Where are you?' Pete asked.

Curly's voice sounded odd, but Pete couldn't quite put his trotter on how or why. 'There was nothing at the salon, Captain,'

Curly said, 'so I . . . went back to the planes.'

'What?' said Pete in surprise. 'Why didn't you wake me u— Er, why didn't you come and get me?'

'Can't explain now!' blurted Curly. 'I'm . . . *busy* with something!'

'You can't act this way on a mission,' said Pete gently. 'It's against the rules, and I know you study the *PiPs Rules and Regulations* as bedtime reading.'

There was no answer, and Pete realized that the line was dead. Had Curly hung up? Pete tried calling back, but the trainee's phone was off now.

That's odd, thought Pete. He was relieved when his phone rang again seconds later.

'Curly?' he said.

But it wasn't the trainee, it was Brian.

'You'd better come to the palace quickly,' the medic said. 'Tammy's acting a bit . . . oddly.'

She's not the only one, thought Pete. He
really wanted to go back to the planes and
check on Curly.

But then Brian added, 'Can you come
NOW, Captain?' and Pete realized that this
was serious.

'I'll be right there.'

'What about Curly?' asked Brian.

'He's not coming,' said Pete with a frown.
'I guess he's all tied up with something.'

CHAPTER 7:

Sheep-Dip of Death

Curly *was* all tied up with something – a piece of rope, to be exact. It was tied round his middle and suspended from the ceiling. Curly was hanging by it, right over a huge vat of green liquid.

Wolfman had been holding the trainee's phone up so the pig could speak into it.

'You said your lines well,' Wolfman grinned.

'That's because I didn't want to get dropped into THAT stuff!' Curly looked down. The sign on the vat said 'Sheep-Dip'. 'That isn't normal sheep-dip, is it?'

Wolfman's huge grin grew. 'Well . . . it *would* get rid of any nasty ticks and fleas you might have. It would also get rid of everything else, apart from your skeleton.' As a demonstration, he dropped Curly's phone into the liquid, which bubbled and fizzed in a way that made Curly's stomach do the same.

'I had a lot of credit left on that phone,' complained Curly. Then again, at the moment Curly had bigger problems than losing phone minutes and unlimited texting.

'Why didn't you just hypnotize me?' he asked.

Wolfman paused. 'You mean, why have I suspended you over

the extra-strong, special-recipe Sheep-Dip of Death? Why have I used a weak bit of rope that may only hold your weight for half an hour?' He shrugged. 'I'm just *bad*, I suppose. Maybe my pack bullied me when I was a cub? Maybe I just hate farm animals like you and all these stupid bleating sheep.'

'Are you going to try to steal the Golden Fleece again?' asked Curly.

Wolfman smirked and shook his shaggy head. 'Getting the Golden Fleece is just the start of my plans, little piggy . . .'

Pete expected to find Brian and Tammy making preparations at Flockingham Palace. He *didn't* expect to find Brian scribbling furiously in a notebook while wearing a riot helmet and body armour. There was a small digital recorder on the table between him and Tammy.

'Er, what's going on?' Pete asked.

'Allow me to demonstrate,' said Brian. 'Step well back.'

'I don't think we need to show him, Brian,' said Tammy. 'We should –'

But Brian had already pressed a button on the recorder. It played an audio clip of a Sheep Island state ceremony. Over the noise of the band and the crowd in the background, Pete heard a sheep say, 'We are delighted to welcome Her Royal Majesty, Queen Baabara.'

With a sudden jerk, Tammy got to her feet.

'Notice the subject's blank stare,' commented Brian. 'Having seen that there are no weapons to hand, she will proceed to attack with her bare trotters.'

The mechanic started walking mechanically towards Pete.

'Attack?' said Pete.

It was clear that Tammy didn't recognize

him. It was also clear she didn't intend to hug him.

'What are you doing, Tammy? Pack it in.'

'And now, observe as I play the second clip,' said Brian calmly. He pushed another button on the recorder . . . and nothing happened.

'Oh, um, I think the batteries have run out!' he said.

Meanwhile Tammy was saying, 'Kill the pig!' and reaching for Pete's neck. The captain ducked out of her grasp and legged it around the room.

Brian was fumbling in his pockets. 'Now – does this take AA or AAA batteries?' he mumbled. 'I always get them mixed up . . .'

'Hurry up!' yelled Pete, who was already on his second circuit of the room, with Tammy close behind.

Brian reached for a battery, and promptly dropped it. It rolled under the table. By the

time he had retrieved it, Tammy
had caught up with the captain
and was giving him a good
throttling.

Brian slotted the batteries in.
'Oops, wrong way round!'

'Qui–i–i–ick!'

Finally Brian pushed the right
button and the second audio clip
played. This one was from a speech
given by the Queen of Sheep Island
herself. Again Pete could tell it was

a large public affair because he could
hear music and crowd noise. On the
clip, Queen Baabara was saying, 'We
are not amused to learn of the Sheep
Island team's poor results in the Animal
Paradise Inter-island Quiz.'

Instantly Tammy stopped. She pulled
her trotters away and said sheepishly,
'Oh, sorry, Pete.'

'So, what conclusions do you draw
from our little experiment, Captain?'
asked Brian.

Pete thought it over. 'Well, firstly, if there's a battery to change, we should never ask you, Brian. And secondly . . . what just happened?'

'How much do you know about hypnotism?' said Brian.

'HYPNOTISM?' repeated Pete.

'It's a fascinating topic,' said Brian. 'You see, the mammalian brain consists of two –'

Tammy held up a trotter. 'Skip the brain science, Bri. The important bit is this: someone has gone and hypnotized me.'

'But you're acting normally,' said Pete.

'Ah, that's the interesting bit.' Brian pushed his glasses up his snout. 'Tammy's been brain-trained. She's under a hypnotic spell. She acts perfectly normally . . . until she hears the trigger words. Then she turns into a killing machine – specifically, a *pig*-killing machine.'

'So what are these trigger words?' asked Pete.

'It took me a while to work them out,'

said Brian proudly. 'I had to reconstruct the conditions that first set Tammy off. It was a painful process of trial and error.' He gave his riot helmet a grateful tap. 'Finally I worked out that the trigger words are –'

'Don't say them!' cried Pete.

Brian smiled. 'It's OK. I soon worked out that the trigger only works if a sheep is speaking. That's why I've used audio clips from my *Favourite Royal Speeches* CD. It seems the trigger words are "Royal Majesty, Queen Baabara" and the Off switch is "We are not amused".'

'That's incredible!' breathed Pete.

'What, that one of us should be hypnotized like this?' asked Tammy.

'No . . . that Brian goes around with a *Favourite Royal Speeches* CD in his backpack.'

Pete thought about how this new development affected the PiPs operation. 'Tammy, you shouldn't take part in the rest of the mission. It's too risky – what if you hear the trigger words again?'

'I don't think that will be necessary. I know a little about hypnosis myself,' said Brian, who had read *The Ultimate Guide to Hypnotizing Your Friends and Family for Financial Gain* from cover to cover. 'Now we've identified the trigger words, I'm confident I can reverse the effects.'

Pete had to think fast on his trotters. He was worried about Curly. What if the trainee had been hypnotized too? What if he was in danger? But the mission was the most important thing. As PiPs captain, it was his job to make sure they completed it. They'd just have to check on Curly afterwards.

'OK,' he said. 'Is the decoy fleece ready?'

Tammy pointed at a second fleece that had been hastily spray-painted gold.

'Good,' said Pete. 'So you two will ride in

the royal limo with the fake. You'll be the decoy.' He grabbed the real Golden Fleece. 'Which means all I need to do is deliver Her Majesty to the Houses of Baaliament.'

As he hung perilously over the deadly sheep-dip, there wasn't much for Curly to do except watch Wolfman carrying out his wicked plans.

Actually he wasn't being all that wicked at the moment; he was wheeling a TV into the room. The wolf switched it on, then moved it to face Curly.

'I bet you're wondering what this is for,' said the wolf. 'The SUSPENSE is probably killing you! Get it? Because you're *suspended* from the ceiling?' Wolfman scowled. 'Why does no one ever appreciate my evil, gloating jokes?'

'I think the clue is in the question,' answered Curly.

The TV was
showing live
coverage from
outside the Houses
of Baaliament,
where a crowd of
sheep was already waiting patiently behind
the barriers. One of the TV commentators
was saying, 'We're coming to you live
from the heart of Woollyhampton, where
today Her Royal Majesty, Queen Baabara,
will officially open the new session of
Baaliament later this afternoon.' The
commentator paused, remembering she
had almost an hour of live television to fill
before anything actually happened.

The other commentator, an elderly ram,
chipped in: 'There's a splendid turn-out
today, and some fine . . . er . . . hats in the
crowd. There's a blue one, and – look! –
there's a nice green one. Erm . . .'

Wolfman was putting his sheep costume on again. He gave Curly a concerned look. 'Is the TV loud enough? I don't want you to miss all the fun.'

Curly sighed – OK, bringing in the TV *had* been a little bit wicked, after all.

'After all, how often do you get to see a wolf become the King of Sheep Island?'

'What?' Curly blinked. 'You're crazy!'

'Why, thank you,' replied Wolfman. And then, with a classic evil laugh, the wolf in sheep's clothing was on his way.

Curly was finally all by himself. He looked around for anything that might help him escape. Every little movement seemed to put even more strain on the rope. If he tried to pull himself up or swing free of the vat, the rope would almost certainly break.

The ewe commentator on TV was still filling in time, saying, 'Oo, look – there's a nice yellow hat. With a little luck, we may spot a red one.'

Curly knew he had to escape before the rope snapped. But what could he do? He had nothing with him apart from his woolly hat and the knitting needles his nan had sent him. Without thinking, Curly nervously plucked a tuft of wool from his fleece costume and rolled it on his tummy. Gradually the fibres twisted together until Curly realized he was holding a piece of yarn in his trotter.

The beginnings of a plan began to form in his brain. He started to pull more and more tufts off his fleece and twist them together. He was making his own yarn! He worked faster and faster – pluck and twist, pluck and twist! When he had enough, he carefully reached for the knitting needles in his back pocket.

Lining up his yarn and casting on, Curly started to knit. His needles flew, clacking together furiously. He felt as if his dear old nan was with him. In his mind he could hear her familiar voice; he knew what she'd say – she'd say, 'Put the kettle on, Curly!' (That's what she always said.)

But Curly could imagine what *else* she would tell him, after she'd had a cuppa; she'd say: 'KNIT, YOUNG CURLY! KNIT LIKE THE WIND!'

Pete was waiting round the back of Flockingham Palace, where there was a small airstrip for Queen Baabara's private jet. The PiPs captain tried to concentrate on the afternoon's mission, but he couldn't stop worrying about Curly. As soon as he had delivered the Queen to the Houses of Baaliament, they *had* to find the trainee PiP.

A back door of the palace opened – one of dozens – but Queen Baabara didn't appear. It was her son, Prince Larry.

The young prince did his best to look down his nose at Pete, even though the pig was a lot taller.

'You're Mummy's pilot, then?' Larry demanded.

'That's me, kid,' said Pete.

'I am the future King of Sheep Island!' snapped Prince Larry. 'Address me properly!'

Pete shrugged. 'OK – that's me, Lambchops.'

Anger flashed in the prince's eyes, but then his video phone rang and the look turned to one of sly triumph. He checked the screen and smirked.

'It's for you,' he said.

'I doubt it,' replied Pete.

'No, really,' insisted Prince Larry. 'It's something to do with your little friend . . . What's his name? Curly?'

Pete whirled round. 'How do you know about Curly? Give that to me!' He snatched the phone and stared at the screen. 'What IS this?'

Two yellow eyes were staring up at him from the video phone.

'Look into my eyes,' said a deep voice. 'You are feeling sleepy.'

'Your little hypnosis trick won't work on me, pal!' Pete spat defiantly. Then he added, 'ZZZZZZZZZZZZ!' He was snoring softly.

'Now listen carefully,' continued the voice on the phone.

CHAPTER 8:

Let Your Inner Piglet Fly!

When Queen Baabara came out to board the royal jet, Pete had no memory of those hypnotic yellow eyes on the phone screen.

Once the Queen had taken her seat in the luxurious main cabin, Pete got ready for take-off. He missed the SkyHog already – the royal jet was bigger, and almost certainly slower and less fun to fly.

He addressed the Queen over the plane's two-way intercom system. 'Do you want some gum, Your Maj? It'll stop your ears popping during take-off.'

'Certainly not!' replied the Queen

crossly. 'The last time we tried that, it took hours for the servants to get the gum out again, and our ears were sticky for weeks afterwards.'

Pete rolled his eyes, then fired up the engines. The plane sped along the runway. Once they were in the air, Pete spoke to the Queen again. 'Here's the plan. We're going to fly out away from the city and do a wide loop round the island. Then we'll fly back in from an unexpected angle. So just sit back, eat some grass and enjoy the ride.'

'We will,' replied the Queen.

The plane had just cleared the city and reached cruising height, when there was a radio signal. Pete assumed it must be Lola and Peregrine checking in with him, but when he clicked the receiver on, all he could hear was a snippet of some boring brass band music.

Something *clicked* in his brain. Pete didn't

know it, but Wolfman had just pulled the hypnotic trigger . . .

Back at PiPs HQ, Lola knew that Pete and the Queen must be in the air by now. She called the royal plane on the radio: 'Hi, Pete – just checking that everything is running smoothly. You know you need to land the plane in front of the Houses of Baaliament at three o'clock exactly, yes? . . . Pete? Do you copy that?'

The radio hissed. Lola tried again: 'Pete, can you hear me? Over.'

Suddenly a voice cried out over the radio, 'No! Don't wanna!'

It sounded a *bit* like Pete, but Lola had never heard the captain speak like this before. He sounded like a toddler speaking in Peter Porker's voice.

'Er, are you feeling OK, Captain?' Lola said.

'I don't wanna play airplanes!' came the strange voice. 'They're stinky and borin'! I wanna play cowboys!'

Lola furrowed her brow. Why was Pete talking like a little piglet?

'Stop messing about, Pete. You're not with your niece and nephew any more. We need to talk about your landing.'

'Not gonna!' cried Pete in his odd new voice.

There weren't many times when Lola was lost for words, but this was one of them.

Peregrine came out of his office now and gripped the microphone. 'Snap out of it, Captain!' he exclaimed. 'And that's an order!'

The Wing Commander and the radio operator listened in amazement to the sound coming out of the radio.

'Is he . . . crying?' asked Lola.

Pete's voice spoke again: 'I don't like

you! You're a big stinky and my mum says I shouldn't even play with you coz you've got nits, so NYAH-NYAH-NY-NYAH-NYAH!'

Peregrine's face went purple with fury. 'Why, you –' he began to splutter, but Lola tugged on his arm. She covered the mike with a trotter and hissed, 'I don't think he's joking. Something's wrong! It's like he's reverted to being a four-year-old piglet. This is terrible!'

Peregrine furrowed his brow. 'You're right! Four IS a particularly annoying age.' Peregrine had found Pete's nephew and niece bad enough yesterday evening – they had complained endlessly about his game of *Clean the Base until it's Spick and Span*.

But Lola had a grim look. 'I don't think you understand. I mean – children of four can't usually fly planes, can they?'

'Oh,' said Peregrine, realizing what she meant. 'Oh dear.'

Lola spoke slowly and gently into the microphone. 'Pete, are you there?'

Pete's childish voice came over the airwaves. 'My name's Little Petey.'

'OK then – Little Petey. We're going to play a *game*. Can you be a big boy and do that for me?'

'Will I get a sherbet lolly?' asked Little Petey. 'I like sherbet lollies! This one time I eated fifty and then I sicked up on the floor. It were brilliant.'

'We don't care about that!' snapped

Peregrine crossly. 'Just listen to your instructions!'

Little Petey sounded tearful again. 'I don't like that pig, he's poo-ey!'

Lola shooed Peregrine away from the mike and said, 'That's OK, the pooey pig's gone now. Listen, Little Petey, can you look on the panel in front of you for a button that says AUTOPILOT?'

There was silence, then a small voice said, 'I can read only two words – CAT and BUM.'

Suddenly a new voice came over the radio: 'What on earth is going on? We are having an awfully bumpy ride back there.' It was Queen Baabara! She must have unbuckled herself and come to the cockpit to complain.

'Your Majesty, you have to help!' gasped Lola with relief. 'Can you see a button that says AUTOPILOT?'

'Hmm,' came the Queen's voice. 'And

what letter does this word begin with exactly?'

Lola flicked a nervous glance at Peregrine. 'A,' she said.

'Hmm, of course . . . and just remind us what shape this letter "A" is . . .?'

'It's like . . . a tent with a crossbar!' Peregrine said quickly.

'Ah, here!' replied the Queen's voice. 'One has it!' There was a *CLICK*!

The next moment they heard a recorded voice: 'If you are hearing this message, you may be experiencing technical problems with your Ace Super-Safe Autopilot. We

apologize for any inconvenience. Have a
super day, and thank you for choosing an
Ace product!'

Lola and Peregrine looked glumly at each
other. With no autopilot, the only chance
was to land the plane manually.

'But there's a pig with the mind of a four-
year-old at the controls,' said Peregrine.

'Don't forget the Queen,' Lola reminded
him.

'OK, there's a pig AND a sheep with the
mind of a four-year-old at the controls.'
Peregrine drew a heavy breath. 'They're
doomed!'

There was a pause, then the Queen's voice
piped up again. 'We can hear everything
you're saying.'

Peregrine blushed and sank down into a
chair.

Lola spoke again into the radio: 'OK, just
have a look ahead and tell me what you see.'

There was a long pause, then the Queen said, 'It's rather pretty, actually. We can see blue skies and fluffy clouds.'

'Oo, that cloud looks like a chicken!' chortled Little Petey. 'An' that one looks like a choo choo! An' *that* one looks like a cat's bu–'

'Why yes!' replied the Queen delightedly. 'And that big grey one looks like a giant pyramid! Look, we're heading right for it.'

'What?' Peregrine jumped up and shouted over the radio in alarm. 'That isn't a cloud! That's a *MOUNTAIN*!'

★ ★ ★

Meanwhile at Wolfie T. Wolfman's secret
lair underneath the SHEAR DELIGHT
shearing salon, Curly knitted as if his life
depended upon it . . . which it did. The rope
that held him over the bubbling vat was
making some alarming noises, as if it would
snap any moment now.

Curly looked at the knitting he had
managed so far – the scarf was nothing to
speak of as a fashion item; it was long and
stringy and he had dropped lots of stitches.
But right now Curly had other things on his
mind than looking trendy.

On the TV, the sheep reporter was saying,
'And at last the royal limousine sets off
from Flockingham Palace on its way to the
Houses of Baaliament. Thank goodness.'
The screen showed a long black car making
its way along the route lined with sheep on
either side, all bleating their support. It was

impossible to see inside the tinted windows, but a single gloved hand waved to the crowd.

Curly knotted the end of the scarf into a loop. His only hope of escape lay in hooking this over the light fixture on the ceiling.

He counted to three, and hurled the loop.

It missed, and he only just managed to save it from going into the sheep-dip below. The rope holding him began to creak. Ignoring this, Curly tried once more.

He came closer this time, but again the looped end of the scarf didn't catch.

The rope holding Curly jerked as another strand snapped. He glanced up to see that he was hanging by a thread. It was now or never!

What would his dear old nan tell him? She'd probably say, 'Stay calm and just DO IT, young Curly . . . and then put the kettle on. I'm parched.'

With these words of wisdom ringing in his ears, Curly let fly the home-made rescue-scarf one last time. It hooked on to the light fixture, but Curly had no time to breathe a sigh of relief because at the same instant the rope holding him finally broke.

Curly plummeted towards the deadly sheep-dip. But as soon as the

scarf reached its full extension, he began to swing forward. The wool stretched under the strain, but Curly was a fine knitter – he had been taught by a master – and the scarf held firm. As soon as he was clear of the vat's edge, he let go and dropped safely to the floor.

He was free! He untied the rest of the rope from round his waist. Now he just had to find his way out.

It was only then that he realized someone was watching him. It was a sheep, but it didn't look like one of Wolfman's hypnotized rams.

'Hello?' said Curly.

The sheep pulled a face. 'That's "Hello, Your Highness", actually,' said Prince Larry.

CHAPTER 9:
The Sheep Who Would Be King

Prince Larry pulled out his mobile phone. His hoof hovered over the buttons.

'Who are you calling?' asked Curly.

'Wolfman, of course! We can't let an interfering pig like you ruin our plan!' said Prince Larry crossly. 'Why didn't you just stay put until it was all over?'

'I didn't fancy dying,' said Curly flatly.

Prince Larry's eyes flickered to the snapped rope and the bubbling vat. It was clear he hadn't expected things to get this serious.

'Anyway,' pressed Curly, 'why are you

going along with Wolfman's plan?'

The prince looked sheepish. 'I hired
Wolfman to steal the Golden Fleece.'

'You! But why?'

Anger and shame shone in the prince's
eyes. 'My mummy has been Queen of
this island for years,' he spat, 'and she'll be
Queen for years to come. So what about
me? What do *I* get to do? Nothing! Nothing
but wait! I was in the army for a while,
but I hated it. So I spend all my time on
games and hobbies. I can play four musical
instruments and I'm a world expert at tiddly
winks. But I don't want any of that. I want
to be King! I want it now!'

'And how will stealing the Fleece help?'
asked Curly.

Larry sighed. 'There will be public outrage
when the Fleece is taken. Sheep will call for
the Queen to stand down. And then I, Prince
Larry, will step forward with the Fleece! I

shall be the hero of the day! Everyone will want me on the throne. Me! Mummy will have to go along with it, and then it will be King *Larry* sitting on the throne!'

Curly didn't want to set the prince off on another tantrum, so he spoke gently. 'What makes you think Wolfman was telling you the truth?' He pointed at the royal limo on the TV screen.

The two TV commentators were clearly struggling. 'It's a little more difficult than usual to glimpse the Queen this year,' said the old ram.

'But we have got a good shot of her waving hand,' said the ewe. 'And she appears to be holding a doughnut. That's a royal first!'

'As the royal limousine rounds the final corner, the band strikes up the music,' said the ram commentator.

'This is odd,' said the ewe. 'The car has

stopped and the Queen appears to be ...
attacking her driver!'

'Now the driver is throwing open his door
and running. If I'm not mistaken, he's a pig!'
said the ram.

'Most unusual!' said the ewe. 'And look,
Her Royal Majesty the Queen is also out
of the car and running after him. She is,
of course, wearing the traditional Golden
Fleece. And, in a bold fashion move, she
seems to have set aside her usual sensible
shoes in favour of gigantic brown boots.'

RAMAVISION

To Curly it was obvious that this wasn't Queen Baabara at all – it was Tammy, and she was clearly trying to clobber Brian.

'Wonderful to see our monarch is such a good runner, even at her age,' the ram commentator was saying. 'I expect she'll catch that pig soon!'

'Must be all the grass she eats,' said the ewe commentator. 'Um . . . I think maybe we ought to go to some adverts now.'

But suddenly a *gigantic* sheep pushed his way to the reporters' side. 'I don't think so,' he growled, and then he looked straight into the camera. Curly would recognize those yellow eyes anywhere. It was Wolfman! The wolf's hypnotic eyes seemed to fill the screen.

'Sheep of Sheep Island, you are feeling oh-so-sleepy!'

'Don't listen!' shouted Curly. 'He's trying to hypnotize everyone on the island!' He

covered the prince's eyes and shouted 'LA
LA LA LA LA!'

Curly himself heard Wolfman's words, but
luckily the wolf had addressed them only
to the *sheep* on the island: 'Find the Pigs in
Planes and find the royals, and bring them
to me . . . dead or alive!'

All over the island, thousands of sheep in
front of their TVs got to their feet. It was the
same story along the packed streets between
Flockingham Palace and the Houses of
Baaliament, where huge screens had been
put up for the TV broadcast.

'What is he *doing*?' asked Prince Larry,
realizing the plot was going terribly wrong.

'Wolfman has a plan of his own,' said
Curly. 'He wants to become the King of
Sheep Island himself! We have to try to stop
him.'

Larry made an effort to stop panicking.
'There is *one* way,' he said, 'but we have to

get to Baaliament Square. And how are we going to do *that*?'

Curly hadn't given up hope yet. 'Come with me,' he told the prince. 'I've got an idea. We're going upstairs to get you some haircare products!'

Miles from Woollyhampton, the *real* Queen Baabara was in the co-pilot's seat of the royal jet, zooming right towards a mountain.

'Pull back!' screamed Peregrine over the radio. 'Pull back on the yoke!'

Queen Baabara looked crossly at the many controls. 'Yolk? As in egg yolk? We have simply no idea *what* you are saying.'

'It's the stick thing in front of the pilot's seat!'

'Mr Sticky!' shouted Little Petey. He grabbed the yoke and yanked back hard. The nose of the plane lifted and it cleared

the summit of the mountain – *just*.
The plane continued to climb
almost vertically, hurtling up
through the clouds like a rocket.

'WHEEEEEEEEEEEE!' cried
Little Petey.

'EEEEEEEEEEEEEEK!' cried
Queen Baabara.

'Too steep!' shouted Lola in
alarm at the sound of the engine
noise. 'You're going to stall! Push
the yoke . . . push *Mr Sticky*
forward, just a bit!'

Little Petey shoved the yoke forward. The engines screamed as the plane began to plummet towards the ground in an almost vertical dive.

'Too much!' yelled Lola. 'Pull back! Pull back!'

'We are about to lose our grass!' wailed the Queen, gripping the sides of her chair.

But Little Petey wasn't wailing – he was starting to laugh.

Both Lola and Peregrine huddled round the radio and listened to the chilling sound of that childlike laugh over the airwaves.

And then everything went quiet.

'Little Petey? Your Majesty? Are you still there?'

The only sound was the steady hiss of air.

'Pete, can you hear us?' cried Peregrine.

Still no answer.

'Maybe they bumped the panel radio

by accident and turned it off?' Lola said hopefully.

But even if that was true, what were they going to do now? Neither Queen Baabara nor Peter Porker in his current condition seemed able to fly a plane. There was no chance of telling them what to do over the radio.

They were on their own.

CHAPTER 10:

Bushed

Brian threw a glance over his shoulder. He was out of breath and he was getting a stitch, but he didn't dare slow down – not with Tammy, still wearing the fake spray-painted Golden Fleece, striding after him on her mission to clobber him with a spanner.

But then he heard the thunder of many hoofsteps from ahead. He looked in the direction of the Houses of Baaliament to see hundreds of sheep, all heading towards him. The look in their blank eyes was as scary as Tammy's and, like hers, those blank eyes all seemed to be pointed at him. The flock of sheep surged forward like an unstoppable woollen tidal wave.

Not wanting that wave to crash down upon him, Brian looked around quickly for somewhere to hide. The only place he could see was a small green bush off to the side of the road. With the crowd of mindless sheep almost upon him, Brian leapt to the side and tucked himself behind the bush. He squeezed his eyes shut.

The wall of sheep crashed right into Tammy, pushing her back. They didn't pay any attention to her because she was still wearing the fake fleece. They just thought she was a sheep. What they were after was a pig, but they had no idea where he had gone.

'Brian!' said a familiar voice. 'Fancy meeting you here!'

The medical officer opened his eyes. Curly was crouching behind the little green bush too!

'And this is Prince Larry,' added the
trainee PiP.

'We've already met,' said the little green
bush. 'At the Palace. Only I wasn't a bush
then.'

'Prince Larry?' said Brian, looking closely
at the woolly green shape in front of him.

Curly quickly explained – he had used
the green wool-dye from the shearing salon
to disguise the prince. Instead of just adding

highlights as the bottle suggested, he had sprayed the entire contents on the young royal's fluffed-up fleece.

'There were sheep looking for us the whole way here,' Curly said, 'but every time one got close, Prince Larry just crouched down and they thought he was a bush!' He pointed to where the sheep were milling about. 'What about Tammy?'

'I don't know,' said Brian. 'She didn't hear the trigger words, so I don't know why she attacked again.'

'It's because the trigger wasn't *words*,' said Prince Larry.

'What do you mean?'

'I'll show you . . .' said the little green bush. 'But we have to get closer to Baaliament Square.'

They began to move in the right direction, making sure at all times that Larry was between the two pigs and the

crowd of mindlessly bleating
sheep. It was slow going, but
finally they were close to the
square.

Wolfman was standing on the
Baaliament steps issuing orders to a
group of rams. Sheep were still milling
about everywhere.

'I need to get to the other side of
the square,' Larry said.

'Impossible!' said Brian. 'There
are sheep everywhere. We'll never
make it without being seen.'

Curly didn't say
anything; this was a
time for action. He
charged out into the
open, shouting at
the top of his voice,
'OINK! OINK! I'm
a pig! Come and get

me! OINK! I roll around in the mud
and eat too much!'

Brian saw what the trainee PiP
was doing – causing a diversion!
The medic ran out too, shouting,
'I do not believe in simple animal
stereotypes . . . but I too am a
pig!'

From every part of Baaliament
Square, sheep turned and began
to murmur, 'Baa! Baa! Get the
pigs!' Others joined in as they heard
this chant, until there was a huge
army of hypnotized
sheep shuffling towards
the two pigs.

'What now?' cried
Brian.

'Er . . . leg
it!' said Curly,
who hadn't really

thought this far ahead.

Meanwhile Prince Larry was charging across the square towards the bandstand area. He was no longer acting much like a bush, unless it was a rare form of sprinting bush. He hopped over one crowd barrier, then another . . .

Then he ran straight into something and rebounded on to his bushy behind.

He looked up and realized that what he had run into was Wolfman. The wolf wasn't fooled by the prince's bush disguise.

'Just look at you,' he sneered, 'pretending to be a bush! You don't deserve to be a prince, let alone a king! And your mother doesn't deserve to be Queen either! It's time for a change around here . . . What this island needs is King Wolfie on the throne! And with the entire country under my hypnotic spell, who's going to stop me?'

Prince Larry's bottom lip began to wobble.

'Oh, dear,' grinned Wolfman. 'You've made quite a mess. Look – my sheep army has caught up with your two piggy friends. I shouldn't be surprised if they trample them. I'm afraid this time your mummy can't just drop in and make this mess all better. I'm afraid –'

Wolfman paused because he could hear something – a plane! He looked up in disbelief. It was the royal jet! But how? He had personally turned the pilot back to the age of four. How could a four-year-old fly a plane?

But he didn't have long to wonder. Here the plane was, flying in over Woollyhampton and coming his way!

Inside the plane, Little Petey Porker stuck out his tongue in concentration.

'You are doing jolly well.' Queen Baabara patted him on the head. 'Good boy! But kindly refrain from picking your nose in front of royalty.'

'I'm not pickin' me nose!' cried Little Petey. 'I've got an itch in me brain!'

They had lost the radio link with PiPs base, but he didn't care. Pete had gone back to an age when he wasn't able to read, or tie his shoelaces, or ride a bike without training wheels.

But he could *fly*.

It just came naturally; it was in his blood. He *instinctively* knew just when to ease back on the yoke, when to nudge the throttle forward or backwards.

Pete was a natural-born flyer.

Ahead of them they could see the landmark building of the Houses of Baaliament.

'That is where we wish you to land,' the Queen informed him.

Little Petey gave the sort of cheeky

toddler grin that looks a bit weird on a full-grown pig. Humming 'I'm a Little Poopot' under his breath, he pulled back the throttle and pushed forward on the yoke. The plane's nose pointed gently downwards as it went into its descent.

However, although Little Petey had a natural talent for flying, he didn't know about all the many controls. He didn't know, for example, about lowering the landing gear.

With no wheels down, the first part of the plane that touched the ground was the fuselage. There was a dreadful sound of metal scraping against concrete. It got louder as the entire plane touched down. As it scraped forward along the road, showers of sparks flew out from either side.

Inside the cockpit, Queen Baabara in the co-pilot's seat had her hooves over her eyes, but Little Petey struggled to hold on

to the controls. He could see the Houses of
Baaliament straight ahead.

Acting on gut feeling alone, he jerked the
controls to one side. The plane went into
a final spin as its tail end came swinging
round . . . right towards the spot where
Wolfman and Prince Larry were standing.

Wolfman sprang back to safety. The

plane had almost come to a stop, but
not before the tail end slammed into
Prince Larry. It shot the green ram into
the air, right towards the bandstand.

'WAAAAAAAAAAAAAAAAAAAAAH!'

He landed end-first in an abandoned
tuba. Staggering shakily to his feet, he
grabbed one of the trumpets left behind by

the band. Then he straightened up, puckered his lips, and began to play. He was a bit rusty, but the tune was recognizable. It was the last lines of 'Baa, Baa, Royal Sheep'.

As soon as they heard the music, the crowd of sheep surrounding Brian and Curly just stopped in their tracks. They all looked confused. At the front of the group, Tammy looked at the spanner in her hands, and rolled her eyes.

'Not again!' she complained.

Meanwhile, Brian was slapping his head. 'It was the *music*! That was the trigger, not the words! When we were at the Palace, it was the *band practice* outside that triggered you. And the same music was playing in the audio clips we used. It was just chance that the *words* were the same!'

But Curly had more pressing concerns. 'Where's Wolfman?' he asked.

He pushed his way through the crowd

of baffled sheep towards the Houses of Baaliament. Up ahead, he could see Wolfman making use of the general confusion to shove his way back towards the TV cameras. Was he going to try hypnotize the island's sheep all over again?

Wolfman elbowed the two TV commentators aside and stared once more into the lens. His yellow eyes blazed like fire. 'Residents of Sheep Island,' he began, but he didn't manage any more than that. Curly leapt up from behind and jammed his PiPs woolly hat over the top half of Wolfman's head. With his hypnotic eyes out of view, the power was gone.

'Quick!' Curly shouted to the nearby GrassEaters. 'Arrest this wolf!'

The crowd began to cheer. They cheered even louder when Queen Baabara staggered out of the side door of the royal plane. She couldn't walk straight and her crown was on at a funny angle, but she was proudly wearing the real Golden Fleece.

Behind her a large pig came bounding out. He pointed back at the plane. 'Didja see that?' he cried. 'I wanna do it again!'

Once everyone had been de-hypnotized, the Opening of Baaliament went without a hitch.

Back at the Palace afterwards, the Queen listened to her son's confession gravely. 'We believe you have learnt your lesson. Indeed, as a reward for your bravery, we have decided to give you more royal duties.'

'Really, Mummy?'

'Indeed. We are sending you on an official tour of the Sheep Tick Islands.'

This was an island chain to the north where wild sheep roamed across the barren, windswept rocks and hungry sheep ticks roamed across the sheep.

'Thank you, Mummy,' said Prince Larry sheepishly.

Queen Baabara turned to the PiPs. 'As for all of you . . . as a token of our gratitude, you will stay at the Palace for a six-course grass banquet.'

The PiPs shuffled uneasily as they tried to think up excuses. Tammy said she was starting a new pie-only diet, and Pete explained that he had booked a session at the Fry Up tanning salon.

When she saw the panicked look on their faces, the Queen smiled broadly. 'We are most amused.'

Epilogue

Air Chief Marshal Plumpkin's yearly visit
to the PiPs base was almost over, and so far
it had gone really well. As usual, Peregrine
had taken the visitor on a full tour. The
two looked impressive together. As befitted
the highest-ranking officer, the Air Chief
Marshal's tummy was
even larger than
Peregrine's and his
moustache was
even bigger.
Of course,
the Air Chief
Marshal had
also wanted to

meet the PiPs team.

'I received a telephone call from the Queen of Sheep Island,' he told Pete. 'She said to me that you did a fine job yesterday.'

'Thank you, sir.' Pete winked at Peregrine and Lola. 'It was just a matter of finding my inner piglet.'

'Good job, all of you!' Plumpkin turned to the whole team. 'And you all look quite striking in those matching woolly hats, I must say.'

Curly beamed.

There was just time for the Air Chief Marshal to have a light lunch and then his helicopter for the mainland would be ready for take-off. Peregrine was already looking relieved. For once, nothing had gone wrong!

The two senior officers headed for the dining area.

'But what's going to happen when Peregrine has a chocolate biscuit?' asked

Tammy. 'He won't be able to stop himself. And if another button pings off and hits the Air Chief Marshal in the eye, it'll be a disaster again.'

Lola gave a little smile. 'It's not going to happen,' she said. 'Your mission gave me a brilliant idea. I borrowed Brian's book and tried a little hypnotism on the Wing Commander.'

'Are you sure you did it right?'

Lola nodded. 'Oh, yes. As soon as he's offered a chocolate biscuit, that's the trigger. He'll just smile politely and say, "No, thank you." You'll see.'

The team watched through the window as a plate of chocolate biccies was brought to the two officers.

The Air Chief Marshal smiled. 'Well, Oinks-Gruntington, for once I'm nicely surprised by how well everything is running here.' He helped himself to a biccie, then held the plate out. 'Want one yourself?'

As soon as the trigger words were spoken, Peregrine's eyes went blank. Then he hopped up on to his chair and clamped both trotters to his waist.

'Er, Lola?' asked Brian. 'Was anyone else in the room when you were hypnotizing Peregrine?'

'I think Pete was singing to his niece and nephew on the phone,' said Lola. 'Oh. Oh dear . . .'

The Air Chief Marshal watched in open-mouthed astonishment as the Wing Commander began to sing in his booming voice:

'I'm a little poopot,
Short and stout!'

He did all the actions, and he was surprisingly nimble for such a bulky pig.

'Here is my handle
For waving me about.'

The rest of the PiPs watched in horror.
'He must have heard Pete instead of my
instructions!' cried Lola.

Pete was already heading for the door.
'Where are you going?' cried Tammy. 'It's
our duty to do something!'

'Adult pigs have to do their duty,'
explained Pete. 'I'm getting in touch with
my inner piglet . . . and doing a runner!'

The other PiPs thought this over, while
Peregrine's voice floated through the

window behind them:

   'When I get all filled up

   Hear me shout:

   Don't kick me

   Or poo will fly out!'

They had to admit, it was important to get in touch with your inner piglet every once in a while.

'PiPs are GO!' they all shouted, chasing Pete out through the door.

READ MORE OINKCREDIBLY FUNNY ADVENTURES OF THE

Crossword

3. Petey's favourite type of lollies

4. Tammy can't eat chips without this.

7. The Houses of _____.

10. The sound a pig makes!

11. The 'I' in PIAF

12. Pete landed on one of these . . . Ouch!

Down ↓

1. A baby sheep.

2. The slightly grumpy pig.

5. To be a cool pig you must *not* own one of these.

6. One of Curly's hobbies.

8. The colour of the 'Sheep-Dip'.

9. Who stole the Golden Fleece?

★ Turn to page 150 for the answers.

Wordsearch

Find the words opposite hidden in this grid.
(Look carefully – some may be
backwards or diagonal!)

R	O	M	K	P	A	L	A	C	E	P	I
Q	A	H	F	Y	C	E	P	C	K	O	S
C	P	G	P	L	D	R	J	X	G	R	L
K	R	L	L	U	E	F	H	K	U	K	A
Y	I	O	A	V	P	E	Z	M	I	E	N
G	N	L	N	E	A	O	C	U	S	R	D
F	C	A	E	P	X	B	O	E	J	D	V
B	E	S	H	D	V	R	K	P	A	R	Y
N	S	H	E	E	P	D	W	J	O	E	A
W	C	L	Y	P	V	J	Y	K	H	T	O
X	B	G	O	L	D	E	N	L	V	X	H

★Turn to page 150 for the answers.

POOPOT   PALACE

FLEECE   LOLA

PLANE   GOLDEN

ISLAND   PRINCE

PORKER   SHEEP

Word Scramble

Unscramble these words:

1. **ALNWOMF**

2. **GOFKLAMCHIN**

3. **JYEMTAS**

4. **LAMHRAS**

5. **ABARABA**

6. **IPLRCKSE**

7. **NICIMLAR**

8. **TIAANCP**

9. **OYRLA**

10. **HNTYOPIEZ**

★ Turn to page 150 for the answers.

Answers

Crossword

Across and down entries:

```
         ¹L
      ²P  A
³S H E R B E T
      E  M
⁴K E T C H U P
      R
      E
⁵C    G        ⁶K
⁷B A A L I A M E N T    ⁸G
  A   R        I        R
  R   I        T   ⁹W   E
¹⁰O I N K      T   O    E
  A   E        I   L    N
¹²C A C T U S  N   F
  N            G   M
               ¹¹I S L A N D
                   A
                   N
```

Wordsearch

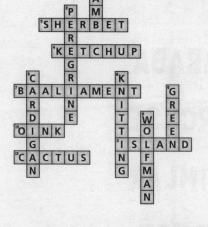

Word Scramble

1. WOLFMAN
2. FLOCKINGHAM
3. MAJESTY
    MARSHAL
6. PRICKLES
7. CRIMINAL
8. CAPTAIN
9. ROYAL
10. HYPNOTIZE